THIS BOOK

belongs to

....

In memory of my dad, who showed me the joy of sport. – B.L.

For Abel and his contagious enthusiasm, with love. - M.R.

Published in 2023 by Welbeck Editions
An imprint of Welbeck Children's Limited,
part of Welbeck Publishing Group.
Based in London and Sydney.
www.welbeckpublishing.com

978-1-80338-043-8

FSC www.fsc.org MIX Paper | Supporting responsible forestry FSC® C104740

Printed in Dongguan, China

10 9 8 7 6 5 4 3 2 1

let's play SOCCER!

Ben Lerwill
Marina Ruiz

WELBECK
EDITIONS

Soccer is the biggest sport in the whole world.

People call it "the beautiful game."

But it's not just for superstars!

To play soccer, we only need two things.

1. A ball.

2. Somewhere to play.

Soccer is played everywhere in the world.

It's played in hot places,

in chilly places,

and in hilly places.

It's even been played in space!

We can play soccer when we're very young...

...and we can play soccer when we're very old!

We can play soccer using a wheelchair...

...or a walker...

...or crutches.

And we can play soccer if we're blind,
using a ball with bells inside.

Playing soccer helps keep us fit and healthy.
We can play it on our own
or with lots of friends.

We can play it early
in the morning...

...or last thing at night.

To play soccer, it doesn't matter
if we're a girl or a boy, or how we look.
It doesn't matter where we live,
or how much money we have.

Soccer is for EVERYONE!

People have played games with balls
for thousands of years.

They played in Ancient Egypt...

...in Ancient China...

...in Ancient Greece...

...and in Ancient Rome.

For a long time, soccer has helped to bring people together.

Even in the middle of World War I, some of the soldiers stopped fighting for a few hours and played soccer with each other!

Today, thousands of millions of people love soccer.
Some of them play every week.
Some of them play every single day!

Some of them don't play at all,
but they still love to watch.

The most important thing about soccer isn't winning or losing.

Soccer is about trying our best,

playing as a team,

and having fun!

LET'S PLAY SOCCER!

Let's talk about SOCCER!

We can play soccer in a park, in a garden, on a beach, in a sports center, and many other places too.

Where's your favorite place to play?

One of the best things about playing soccer is that it gives us exercise. Running around is good for us!

Other sports help to keep us healthy too. Can you think of any other ball games?

On a soccer team, different players have different jobs. The goalkeeper tries to keep the ball from going in the goal.

Defenders try to stop the other team from shooting and scoring.

Midfielders help their teammates by passing and tackling in the middle of the pitch.

Forwards work together to try to score goals.

Which job do you like the best?

Some soccer teams are very famous. They have big stadiums, star players, and millions of fans. Other teams are smaller, but they have lots of local fans.

Do you have a favorite team?

Let's practice our soccer SKILLS!

Can you drop the ball from your hands and kick it high into the air, like a goalkeeper?

How far can you kick it?

You can practice your passing and shooting skills with a friend, by kicking the ball to each other.

Try aiming the ball so that it goes right to your friend's feet!

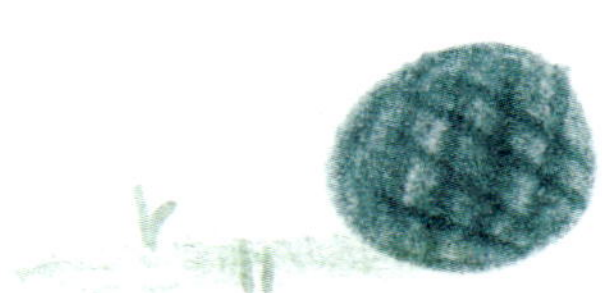

When you keep the ball close to your feet as you move forward, we call this dribbling.

You can practice dribbling by zig zagging between plastic cones, old flowerpots, or even yard toys!

When players score a goal in soccer,
they celebrate because they're happy.
They give high-fives and congratulate each other.
Some even do a little dance!

How would you celebrate
if you scored a goal?